Derrick AND THE Dinosaurs

By Dan Killeen

Happy Fun Books
St. Louis

Published by
Happy Fun Books
St. Louis, MO

Please visit
HappyFunBooks.com

ISBN 978-0-9898474-4-5

Printed in Canada

There once was a boy named Derrick, and he loved dinosaurs.

He loved to play with toy dinosaurs, sometimes invading his sister Becky's room.

He loved to eat like a dinosaur, devouring cupcakes and guzzling root beer.

3

But mostly he loved to roar like a dinosaur.
One day at school, he even got some other kids to roar along with him.

The teacher and principal were not happy with Derrick's trouble making, and neither were his parents when they were called in for a meeting.

Derrick was suspended for the day, which was a real bummer because that was the day of the big school field trip. All the other kids were headed downtown to visit neat places and do fun activities.

Mom and Dad told Derrick he needed to quit all his stomping around and roaring. When they got home, they made him pack up all his dinosaur things and store them in the basement.

No field trip and no more dinosaur stuff - this was not shaping up to be a very good day for young Derrick.

Just then, folks all across town crowded around television sets. The mayor was coming on to make an urgent announcement.

And next, the TV showed three boatloads of ferocious dinosaurs sailing up the Mighty Muddy River!

Derrick and his parents watched the dreadful event unfold before their very eyes.

Radio Rick described the scene as the dinosaurs landed and marched into town,
"*LARGE LIZARDS ARE CAUSING CHAOS IN OUR MODEST METROPOLIS!*"

Derrick ran to his dinosaur stash, put his favorite shirt back on, and tied his bedsheet on like a cape.

I'LL go downtown and check on Becky. I'LL make those dinosaurs behave.

I don't know, Derrick. You're just a little kid.

Yeah, and it's awfully dangerous downtown.

15

As all the other folks scrambled to escape the mayhem,
Derrick ran right into the middle of it.

He rounded the corner to behold a terrible site - dinosaurs playing kickball with a police car!

Then the boisterous bunch gathered together for a triumphant group roar.

Derrick took the opportunity to climb atop the General Grant statue, where he would get the dinosaurs' attention by yelling..

Derrick had never been asked by dinosaurs to go on a romp. It's not why he had come downtown, but the offer was tempting. He paused to consider their invitation.

Come on, kid. What do you say?

It will be cool!

C'mon, Derrick!

Yeah! RAWR!

They crashed the school field trip, which was taking place at the City Museum.

27

Derrick invited his friends to climb aboard and join the rowdy expedition. Soon the kids forgot they were kids and went right along with the dinosaurs.

The gang stormed into the baseball stadium, where the home team was taking on their rivals from Onion City. A few dinosaurs growled at the visitors' dugout, while the rest had a good time running the bases, eating some bats, and greeting the fans.

29

Afterward, they raided the Yummy Yummy Cupcake Factory. Kids and dinosaurs alike gorged on fresh baked cupcakes. It was a sugary sweet experience, but all those cupcakes made the mob thirsty.

So the party shuffled over to the Burpy Root Beer Factory. Everyone swilled lots of cold, frosty root beer and was enjoying themselves, except for Becky. She announced she was going to tell Mom and Dad what Derrick was up to.

Next, the pack occupied the old university, where the dinosaurs feasted on students' homework. Derrick thought it strange that of all the different things the big beasts had eaten that day, they seemed to enjoy homework the most.

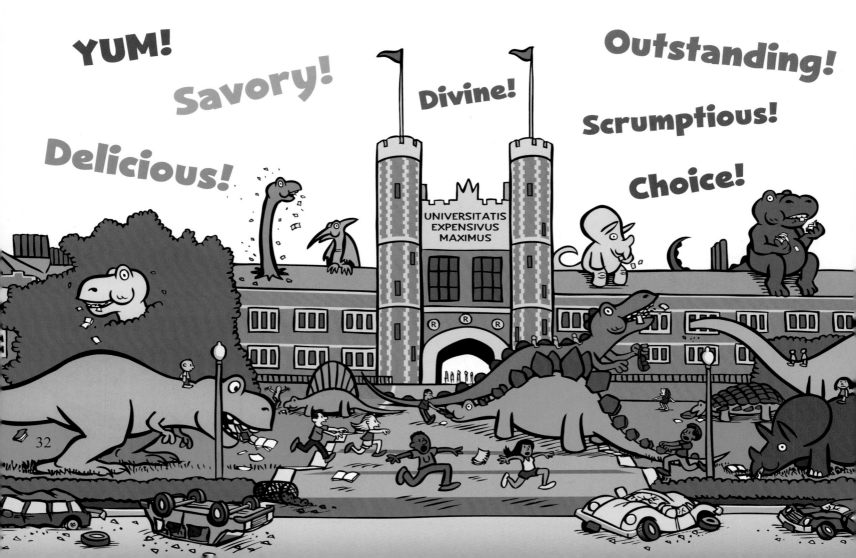

33

35

Derrick and his friends realized they did have it pretty good and so decided to return to their parents.

Just then, the mayor came dashing out from his bunker, pleading with the crowd.

Derrick thought of a plan which required all of his friends' help.

41

The children rode to their school, gathered up all their homework, rode back to the riverfront, and filled the dinosaurs' ships.

And they laid a trail of homework between the ships and where the dinosaurs were. The prehistoric creatures took the bait, munching their way back on to their vessels.

As the dinosaurs chowed down on tasty homework, Derrick and his friends pushed the ships out into the river. The colorful monsters floated downstream, back to their home on Dinosaur Island.

THREE CHEERS FOR DERRICK!
HE IS THE MAN!
OUR TOWN WAS
IN TROUBLE,
BUT HE HAD A PLAN.
TWO HEADACHES GONE!
WE KNEW HE WOULD DELIVER.
HOMEWORK AND DINOSAURS
WE SHOVED INTO THE RIVER!

The mayor awarded Derrick the Medal of Awesomeness
and the key to the city.

That night, Derrick's parents helped him bring all of his fun stuff back into his bedroom. He still loved dinosaurs, but Derrick was happy being a little kid and proud that he had rid the town of those troublesome beasts.

The End